OR IS SOMEONE ELSE THE GENIUS?

HA! PUNY MORTAL! YOU ARE ONLY MY TOOL—THE HANDS I USE TO DRAW WITH. BUT GLOAT IF THAT MAKES YOU HAPPY.

THE BOY IS SO PROUD THAT HE MAKES COPIES OF HIS CREATION TO SHOW OTHERS.

HOW DO YOU LIKE MY NEW COMIC?

WOW! YOU SHOULD SELL THESE!

CAN I SEE? I'LL BUY ONE.

AH-HA-HA-HA-HA! YES! LET THE WHOLE WORLD READ OF MY AMAZING WONDERFULNESS!

LITTLE DO THEY REALIZE MY THOUGHTS WILL INFILTRATE THEIRS, AND SOON THEY WILL ALL KNOW THE GLORY OF ALIEN ERASER!

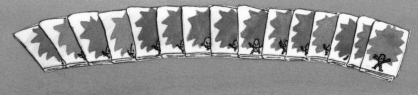

AND SO THE NEWS IS SPREAD. SOON EVERYONE IS EAGER TO READ THE ADVENTURES OF ALIEN ERASER. ARE YOU ONE OF THOSE WAITING FOR THE NEXT INSTALLMENT? WELL, WAIT NO LONGER. TURN THE PAGE FOR MORE ALIEN ERASER—NEW, IMPROVED, AND ABLE TO LEAP TALL PYRAMIDS IN A SINGLE BOUND!

THIS IS MY BOOK FOR WRITING SCIENTIFIC
STUFF IN. I FOUND IT ONE MORNING UNDER
MY PILLOW. I THINK IT WAS A PRESENT FROM
MOM. SHE AND MY DAD ARE BOTH SCIENTISTS.
I'M GOING TO BE ONE, TOO.

MAX DISASTER #2

ALIEN
ERASER
UNRAVELS THE
MYSTERY of the PYRAMIDS

Marissa Moss

Watch out, world! Here I come!

CANDLEWICK PRESS

I like to invent things and do experiments and stuff. But I also want to go beyond science and travel into...

doo-doo-DOO-doo, doo-doo-DOO-doo
THE TWILIGHT ZONE!

Well, at least into the mysteries of ancient Egypt.

Ms. Blodge started us on an Egyptian unit this week! For a brief moment, I almost liked her!

In honor of Egypt, she wore an ankh necklace. At first when she told us about it, I thought she said "honk," like she was blowing her nose. But really she was saying "ankh," the symbol of the life force.

Ms. Blodge is my teacher. The name fits her exactly. She even has a blodgy voice. She's as close as you can come to a mummy and still be alive.

I held my breath while Ms. Blodge assigned partners.

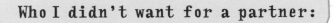

Carmen, because she's so bossy.

WE'RE DOING OUR PROJECT ON KING TUT, AND THAT'S FINAL!

Shawn, because he
always forgets his part.

REMIND ME AGAIN . . . I WAS SUPPOSED TO DO WHAT?

Leon, because he gets food all over his homework.

I CAN TELL WHAT I ATE THE LAST THREE DAYS. IT'S ALL RIGHT HERE ON MY REPORT!

I was super lucky. I got the best possible partner: Omar.

Wow! Usually Ms. Blodge separates us because we're best friends!

It's the Egyptian Life Force working for us. May the ankh be with you!

Now we get to decide if we want to do our project on pyramids, mummies, hieroglyphics, or something else. I don't really care what we do—it's all cool.

Ancient Egypt! I know a thing or two about that!

I read on a cereal box once (a major source of useful information) that Egyptians buried their kings in pyramids because anything put in there doesn't rot.

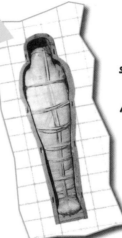

No MUSH, NO FUSS

THE WHOLE IDEA OF MUMMIES IS TO PRESERVE THE DEAD PERSON'S BODY.

THAT WAY, THE DEAD GUY CAN STILL USE HIS ARMS AND LEGS IN THE AFTERLIFE, JUST IN CASE HE WANTS TO CLIMB A TREE OR SOMETHING.

Supposedly, if you put an apple core in the EXACT center of a pyramid that's perfectly aligned from north to south and east to west, it will never get brown and mushy. (Why you would want a crisp, white apple core that lasts forever, I don't know, but that's how you do it.)

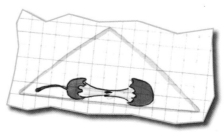

Experiment #1
What happens to different objects stored in the center of a pyramid?

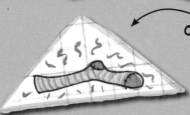

ONE OF KEVIN'S SMELLY SOCKS: WAIT—I DON'T WANT TO PRESERVE THE STINK. I WANT TO GET RID OF IT!

AN EGG: WILL IT HATCH, TURN INTO A ROCK, OR GET EATEN FOR BREAKFAST TWENTY YEARS LATER?

CAFETERIA MEAT LOAF: OOPS! THAT'S ALREADY PETRIFIED. THE PYRAMID WON'T MAKE A DIFFERENCE.

ALIEN ERASER: IT WILL NOT CRUMBLE. IT WILL NOT SELF-DESTRUCT. IT WILL TAKE OVER THE WORLD!

Another time, I read on a bag of chips (another important source of information) that some people think the pyramids were built by aliens who visited Earth a long time ago.

I have definitely found the perfect project for me and Omar. We're going to be the ones to PROVE that theory.

Since my dad's a scientist, I asked him what he thought of pyramid power. Does it really work? Does the pyramid have to be made of something special, or can you use any material to build one?

I had to phone Dad, since now that my parents are separated, he doesn't live with us anymore.

YOU SOUND DISTRACTED. ARE YOU LISTENING OR DOING SOMETHING ELSE?

SPLISH, SPLOSH SOUND OF RUNNING WATER—IS DAD WASHING DISHES? RUNNING A BATH? USING THE TOILET? DOING A SCIENTIFIC EXPERIMENT?

OF COURSE I'M LISTENING.

When you can't see someone, you don't know what they're doing while you talk to them. Sometimes I get the feeling Dad's reading the newspaper or clipping his toenails— anything but really listening.

It seems like Mom doesn't like it when I talk to Dad. I guess she feels left out.

WHY DON'T YOU ASK ME ABOUT PYRAMIDS? I'M A SCIENTIST, TOO, AREN'T I?

Here's why I didn't ask Mom:
As soon as she heard I was studying ancient Egypt, she gave me a HUGE pile of books. The whole point of asking a parent a question is so that you don't have to slog through so many books to find the answer yourself.

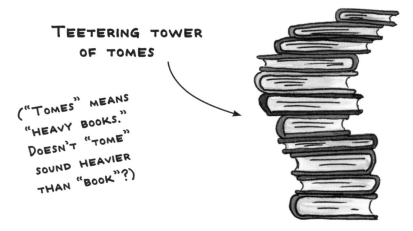

TEETERING TOWER
OF TOMES

("TOMES" MEANS "HEAVY BOOKS." DOESN'T "TOME" SOUND HEAVIER THAN "BOOK"?)

Invention #1
Book-to-Brain Zapper

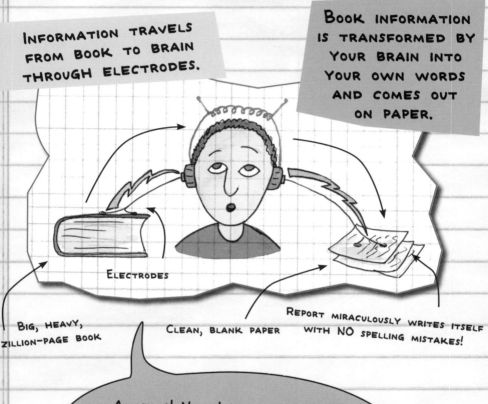

INFORMATION TRAVELS FROM BOOK TO BRAIN THROUGH ELECTRODES.

BOOK INFORMATION IS TRANSFORMED BY YOUR BRAIN INTO YOUR OWN WORDS AND COMES OUT ON PAPER.

ELECTRODES

BIG, HEAVY, ZILLION-PAGE BOOK

CLEAN, BLANK PAPER

REPORT MIRACULOUSLY WRITES ITSELF WITH NO SPELLING MISTAKES!

AMAZING! NOW I KNOW HOW PLATE TECTONICS WORK, WHAT THE CAPITAL OF VENEZUELA IS, HOW MANY YEN THERE ARE TO A DOLLAR, AND WHY YOU SEE LIGHTNING BEFORE YOU HEAR THUNDER.

I should be used to Mom and her books and to Dad living in his own apartment by now, but I'm not. I wish I could turn our house into a giant pyramid and preserve our family the way it used to be before my parents decided they didn't want to be married anymore.

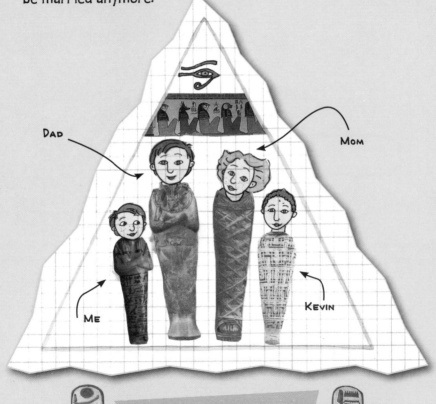

DAD

MOM

ME

KEVIN

THE HAPPY FAMILY—SEALED FOR ETERNITY

At dinner, Mom asked if I needed MORE books about Egypt and pyramids!

ME   MOM   KEVIN

I DON'T NEED BOOKS—I NEED INFORMATION ON ALIENS.

I THOUGHT YOU WERE STUDYING EGYPT, NOT ETs.

MAYBE THE TWO ARE CONNECTED. LOOK—MAX IS SCULPTING HIS MASHED POTATOES INTO A PYRAMID. THAT'S WEIRD, AND HE'S WEIRD.

Then it hit me—Kevin was onto something! I hadn't consciously meant to mold my dinner into a pyramid. The aliens must have MADE me do it! They were sending me a message.

I'm concentrating, concentrating. . . . Does he get it?

But Omar isn't sure an alien message in mashed potatoes is basis enough for a school report. I guess I have to read those books after all to find more proof.

Invention #2
Reading Robot

READS THOUSAND-PAGE BOOKS IN FIVE MINUTES.

BOILS DOWN ALL THE WORDS INTO THE FEW THAT ARE USEFUL TO YOU AND DRIPS THEM INTO A CUP FOR YOU TO DRINK.

Knowledge is now yours!

Actually, some of the books Mom checked out of the library are really interesting. There's one that's all about Egyptian magic.

Priests used incense, smoke, and light to trick people into thinking the gods were speaking to them.

↑
STRONG,
PERFUMEY
SMELLS

↑
COLORED
SMOKE

↑
MIRRORS REFLECT
LIGHT ONTO STATUES.

↑
SUNLIGHT FLOODS INTO
THE TEMPLE DOOR JUST WHEN THE
PRIEST COMES OUT TO CHANT.

OK, it's more science than magic, but it's still cool.

Maybe Omar and I can do an optical trick, like the Egyptian priests did.

Invention #3
Homemade Spying Glass or Periscope

1) FIND ONE REALLY LONG CARDBOARD TUBE OR TWO

   CARDBOARD TUBES, ONE OF WHICH FITS INSIDE THE OTHER.

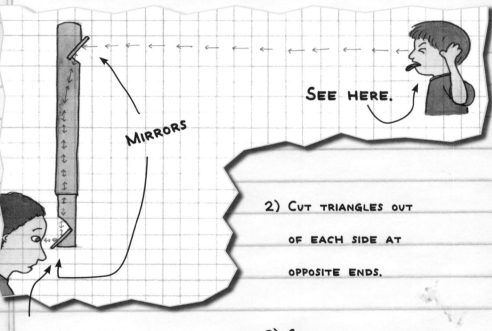

SEE HERE.

MIRRORS

2) CUT TRIANGLES OUT
   OF EACH SIDE AT
   OPPOSITE ENDS.

LOOK HERE.

3) GLUE MIRRORS ONTO THE
   NOTCHES CLOSEST TO
   ENDS OF THE TUBE.

Very interesting—
now if he could just
see clearly!

Invention #4
The Living Staff*

(*THIS ISN'T OUR INVENTION. I READ ABOUT IT IN THE BOOK.)

PRIEST HOLDS STAFF, THEN THROWS IT ONTO THE GROUND, WHERE IT TURNS INTO A SNAKE!

AMAZING! MY STAFF LIVES! SEE IT SLITHER AWAY!

HERE'S THE TRICK: IT WAS A SNAKE ALL ALONG, BUT IT WAS SO COLD, IT WAS SOUND ASLEEP. THROWING IT DOWN WAKES IT UP, AND AWAY IT GOES!

When I showed Omar the book about magic, he got all excited. Now he wants to forget totally about proving aliens built the pyramids and do some kind of magic trick instead. I like magic, too, but I'm not ready to give up on the alien theory yet. I showed Omar my comics.

Yes! Don't forget about me!

ALIEN ERASER

IN

GET THE POINT

For days, Alien Eraser has been meditating.

Ah, I have it! The form has come to me — the perfect shape!

My shape!

It takes many years, but the first pyramid is built, a marvel to behold.

My triumph!

Unfortunately, it is all too popular with pigeons.

Shoo!

Scat!

So, another inspiration comes to him: a point!

Get the point?

And that is how the pyramid took the form we know today.

Drat!

No place to land!

Is that the end of the story? I think not! Find out more in the next episode of ALIEN ERASER!

Omar loved my comic, but it didn't change his mind about the magic thing. Then he said something that made me change MY mind!

The only problem is, some of the ingredients are tricky. Here's what the book said we needed:

WAX (LIKE CANDLES)

FAT (LIKE BUTTER)

DATE WINE

(I'M NOT SURE WHAT THAT'S LIKE)

HONEY

(LIKE THE KIND IN THE BEAR JAR)

BOILED HORN

(LIKE, WHERE WOULD WE GET THIS?)

I love a good magic potion!

Experiment #2
Translating Ancient Love Potion into Modern Concoction

Steps:

1. In microwave, melt together one birthday candle, one stick of butter, and a spoonful of honey.

GOOEY MESS

2. Boil fingernail and toenail clippings in water.

   (I once heard on a nature documentary that a rhino's horn is made of the same stuff as our fingernails, just thicker.)

3. Stir nail clippings and prune juice into melted wax mixture.

   (A prune is like a date. They're both wrinkly and brown and sticky and gross. They're both the kind of thing only grown-ups like.)

Result:

One love potion!

I know it sounds gross to drink toenail juice, but the wisdom of the ancients is not to be ignored.

Saturday morning, I poured two glasses of grape juice and added half the love potion to each. (I strained out the nail clippings first.) It didn't smell TOO bad.

When Dad came to pick up Kevin and me for the weekend, I ran to open the door.

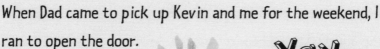

DING DONG!

Yay, it was Dad!

MAX! YOU'RE SURE EAGER TO SEE ME.

I'M GLAD YOU'RE NOT MAD AT ME ANYMORE. DOES THAT MEAN YOU'RE GETTING USED TO ME HAVING MY OWN APARTMENT?

That question was NOT worth answering. I ran to get Mom.
I asked her and Dad to say a toast to wish me good luck on my
Egypt project.

WHAT'S THIS ABOUT A TOAST?

I REMEMBER YOU USED TO HAVE
US DO THAT WHEN YOU WERE LITTLE.
IT'S A GREAT IDEA TO START DOING
THAT AGAIN. EVEN WITH A NEW KIND
OF FAMILY, WE CAN KEEP OLD FAMILY
TRADITIONS, OR INVENT NEW ONES.

It was all turning out to be much easier than I'd expected . . .

... until I went to the kitchen for the juice.

DISASTER!

Kevin had drunk the potion!

MOM, WHAT KIND OF JUICE DID YOU BUY? IT TASTES LIKE OLD SOCKS.

Mom poured all the grape juice down the drain, then we toasted with plain old apple juice.

WHY ARE YOU GLARING AT ME LIKE THAT? STILL GETTING MESSAGES FROM LITTLE GREEN MEN?

ME GIVING KEVIN THE EVIL EYE

Now my parents will never fall in love with each other again, and my Egypt project is ruined.

I had pretty much given up on Egyptian magic when something amazing happened. After we got back home from Dad's place on Sunday night, I overheard Kevin talking to Mom.

OH, MOM, I'M GOING TO THE DANCE FRIDAY NIGHT AFTER ALL, OK?

GREAT! WHAT MADE YOU CHANGE YOUR MIND?

KEVIN AND HIS USUAL BEFORE-BED BOWL OF CEREAL

LUISA SAID SHE'D GO WITH ME.

NEWS FLASH!
MY LOVE POTION WORKED!
KEVIN HAS A GIRLFRIEND!

I can't wait to tell Omar!

Now that Omar and I know the love potion works, we're looking through the book to see what other kinds of magic we can do.

MAGIC CHARMS OR AMULETS

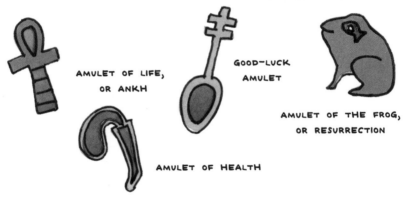

AMULET OF LIFE, OR ANKH

GOOD-LUCK AMULET

AMULET OF THE FROG, OR RESURRECTION

AMULET OF HEALTH

One thing's for sure: we're definitely mixing up a new batch of love potion, and this time I'm going to make sure that Mom and Dad drink it—NO ONE ELSE!

In a way, I guess I'm tricking them. But I'm sure they want to be in love again. They just don't know it.

Is it a good thing or a bad thing to make Mom and Dad fall in love again?

The scale of judgment weighs in with an answer.

The pros win! They're way heavier on the scale than the cons.

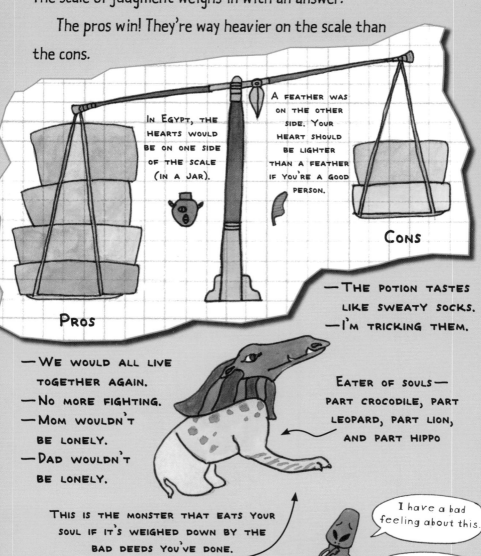

IN EGYPT, THE HEARTS WOULD BE ON ONE SIDE OF THE SCALE (IN A JAR).

A FEATHER WAS ON THE OTHER SIDE. YOUR HEART SHOULD BE LIGHTER THAN A FEATHER IF YOU'RE A GOOD PERSON.

CONS

PROS

— THE POTION TASTES LIKE SWEATY SOCKS.
— I'M TRICKING THEM.

— WE WOULD ALL LIVE TOGETHER AGAIN.
— NO MORE FIGHTING.
— MOM WOULDN'T BE LONELY.
— DAD WOULDN'T BE LONELY.

EATER OF SOULS — PART CROCODILE, PART LEOPARD, PART LION, AND PART HIPPO

THIS IS THE MONSTER THAT EATS YOUR SOUL IF IT'S WEIGHED DOWN BY THE BAD DEEDS YOU'VE DONE.

I have a bad feeling about this.

I never have liked demons.

Now that Kevin has a girlfriend, he's acting strangely nice to me. Is that a side effect of the potion? Whatever the reason, he offered to help with my Egypt project.

WANT ME TO HELP YOU BUILD A PYRAMID? WE COULD MAKE A MODEL OUT OF SUGAR CUBES.

THANKS, BUT I'M NOT MAKING A PYRAMID. I'M WORKING ON SOMETHING ELSE. BUT IF YOU HAVE ANY PROOF THAT ALIENS BUILT THE PYRAMIDS, I'D LOVE TO SEE IT.

ALIENS? WHY DON'T YOU LOOK AT THE TOMB PAINTINGS? THEY SHOW LOTS OF STUFF, MAYBE EVEN ALIENS.

Tomb paintings? What did Kevin think? That the Egyptians drew aliens on their walls? If they had, wouldn't somebody have noticed by now? The love potion may have helped Kevin's love life, but it seemed to have done something bad to his brain.

HE HOGS THE BATHROOM ALL THE TIME NOW. AND HE SPENT HOURS GETTING READY FOR HIS DATE WITH LUISA—EXAMINING EVERY BLOTCH AND PIMPLE AND CHECKING FOR FOOD CAUGHT IN HIS TEETH.

I ALMOST WISHED I COULD UN-LOVE-POTION HIM!
ALL I KNOW IS, LOVE IS DEFINITELY IN THE AIR.

Omar and I agreed: this weekend will be perfect for Mom and Dad. Perfect for love. Perfect for love potions. We mixed up a new batch. This time, we added extra sugar to cover the nail-clipping taste.

Kevin was still sleeping when Dad came to pick us up on Saturday morning, so I knew the potion was safe.

I told Mom and Dad that I had a big test on Monday and needed a toast for good luck.

Mom thought the juice smelled funny, but I told her it was a special healthy mixture I'd invented. How could she say no to that? She didn't! They drank it all! **GLUG GLUG**

GLUG GLUG!

I waited. Mom ran to rinse out her mouth. Dad burped really loudly. Was that it?

Mom went to wake up Kevin, we got our stuff together, and me and Kevin left with Dad.

Could it be magic?

WHY ISN'T THE POTION WORKING?

The whole weekend, Dad didn't talk about Mom ONCE.
Didn't he miss her? Wasn't he falling back in love with her?
I tried some subtle hints at dinner one night.

ROBO-FLORIST

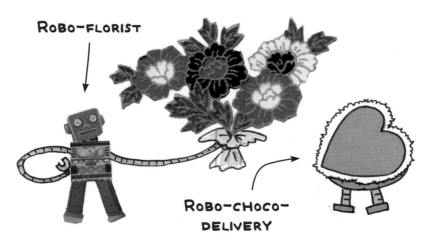

ROBO-CHOCO-
DELIVERY

"Chocolates are a sweet present if you want to tell someone
you like them, right, Dad?" I suggested. "You wouldn't have to
say a word. The candy says it all. Or flowers. Flowers are good."

Kevin kicked me under the table. He thought I was making
fun of him for having a girlfriend. Dad just looked at me like
I was speaking Egyptian, not English.

I called Mom to see if she missed Dad. She didn't. Actually, when I asked, she said, "Are you nuts?"

I don't get it. The potion worked on Kevin. Why not on Mom and Dad?

UM, MOM? DO YOU THINK YOU AND DAD WILL EVER LOVE EACH OTHER AGAIN? I MEAN, YOU LOVED EACH OTHER ONCE, SO YOU KNOW IT'S POSSIBLE.

Mom sighed. She said it doesn't work like that. She'll always be my mom and Dad will always be my dad, and they'll always love me. She said I've just got to accept that they don't want to be married to each other anymore, that they don't love each other anymore.

Maybe I just need to do more research. Between science and magic, there's got to be a way!

Then on Monday, I got terrible news. Kevin broke up with his girlfriend! Already! I guess the potion didn't really work on him, either.

I gave Omar the bad news. He didn't take it very well.

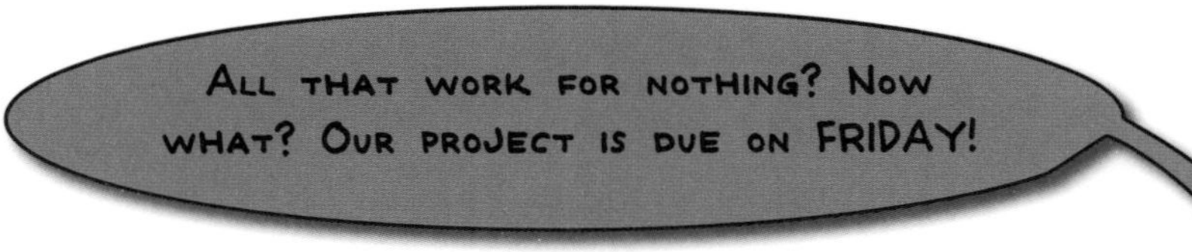
ALL THAT WORK FOR NOTHING? NOW WHAT? OUR PROJECT IS DUE ON FRIDAY!

I told him not to panic, that we can go back to my first idea, that all we need is proof that aliens visited ancient Egypt.

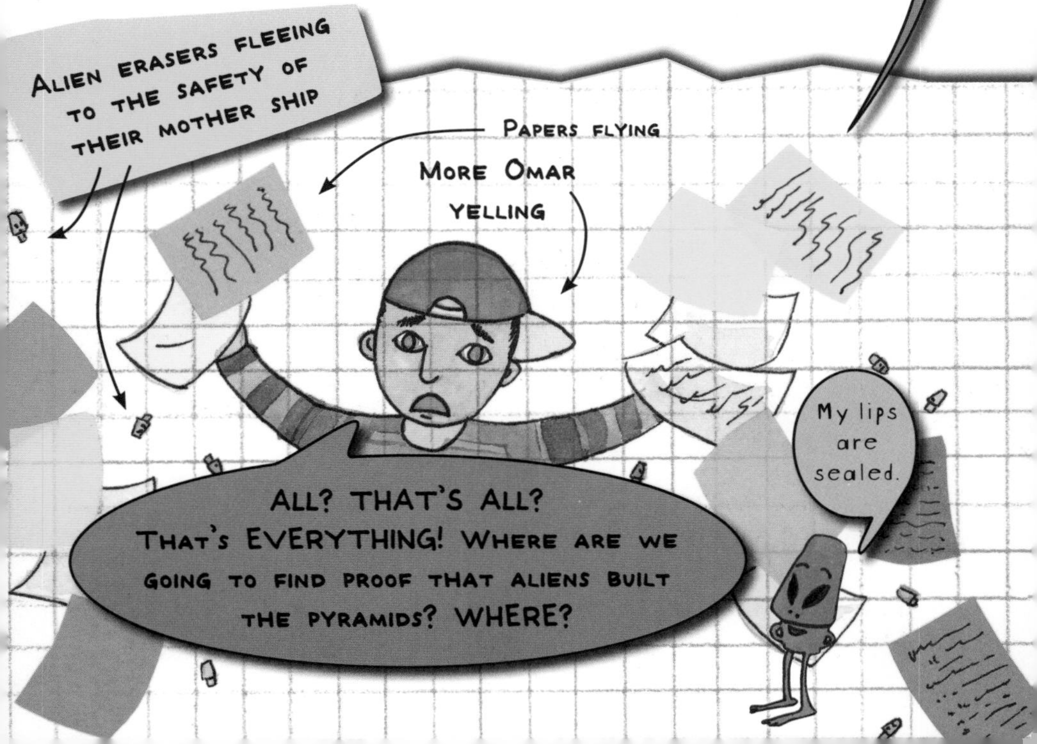
ALIEN ERASERS FLEEING TO THE SAFETY OF THEIR MOTHER SHIP
PAPERS FLYING
MORE OMAR YELLING
ALL? THAT'S ALL? THAT'S EVERYTHING! WHERE ARE WE GOING TO FIND PROOF THAT ALIENS BUILT THE PYRAMIDS? WHERE?
My lips are sealed.

Omar didn't seem too happy with my plan. I don't think he believes that aliens built the pyramids.

"How about we still do our report on potions and charms?" he said. "Even if they don't really work, the Egyptians thought they did."

"OK, that can be our fallback plan," I said, "but give me one more day to find proof of aliens. Just one more day."

I was afraid Omar would flip again, but finally he nodded.

I guess this means I have to go through all those books again.

I read as fast as I could. I just had to find aliens SOMEWHERE!

I could hear Mom yelling at me.

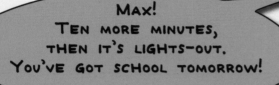

MAX!
TEN MORE MINUTES,
THEN IT'S LIGHTS-OUT.
YOU'VE GOT SCHOOL TOMORROW!

I was frantic. The minutes on the clock had never changed so fast! Then it happened! At **9:27.** precisely,

I found PROOF of ALIENS in ANCIENT EGYPT!

In the tomb of Ramses IV, there are lots of pictures showing the pharaoh conquering his enemies, but this one really stood out!

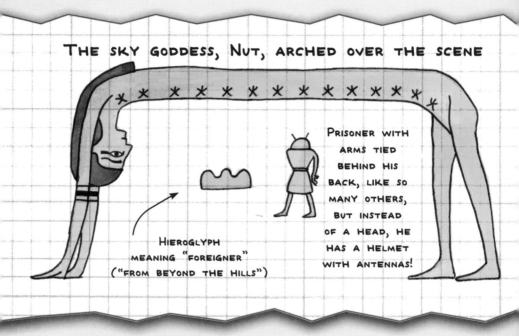

THE SKY GODDESS, NUT, ARCHED OVER THE SCENE

HIEROGLYPH MEANING "FOREIGNER" ("FROM BEYOND THE HILLS")

PRISONER WITH ARMS TIED BEHIND HIS BACK, LIKE SO MANY OTHERS, BUT INSTEAD OF A HEAD, HE HAS A HELMET WITH ANTENNAS!

The other prisoner scenes don't have the sky goddess in them, and they definitely don't have helmet-heads! I read this to mean that Ramses IV defeated a stranger who came from far away—from the sky!

Such a clever boy!

I knew he would figure it out.

I have my proof! Who could refute this? Omar will be astounded, Kevin will be shocked, and Ms. Blodge will be speechless, a miracle in itself!

I RAN TO TO SHOW MOM AND KEVIN.

At school when I told Omar about my discovery, he was so excited that he threw his baseball cap on the roof!

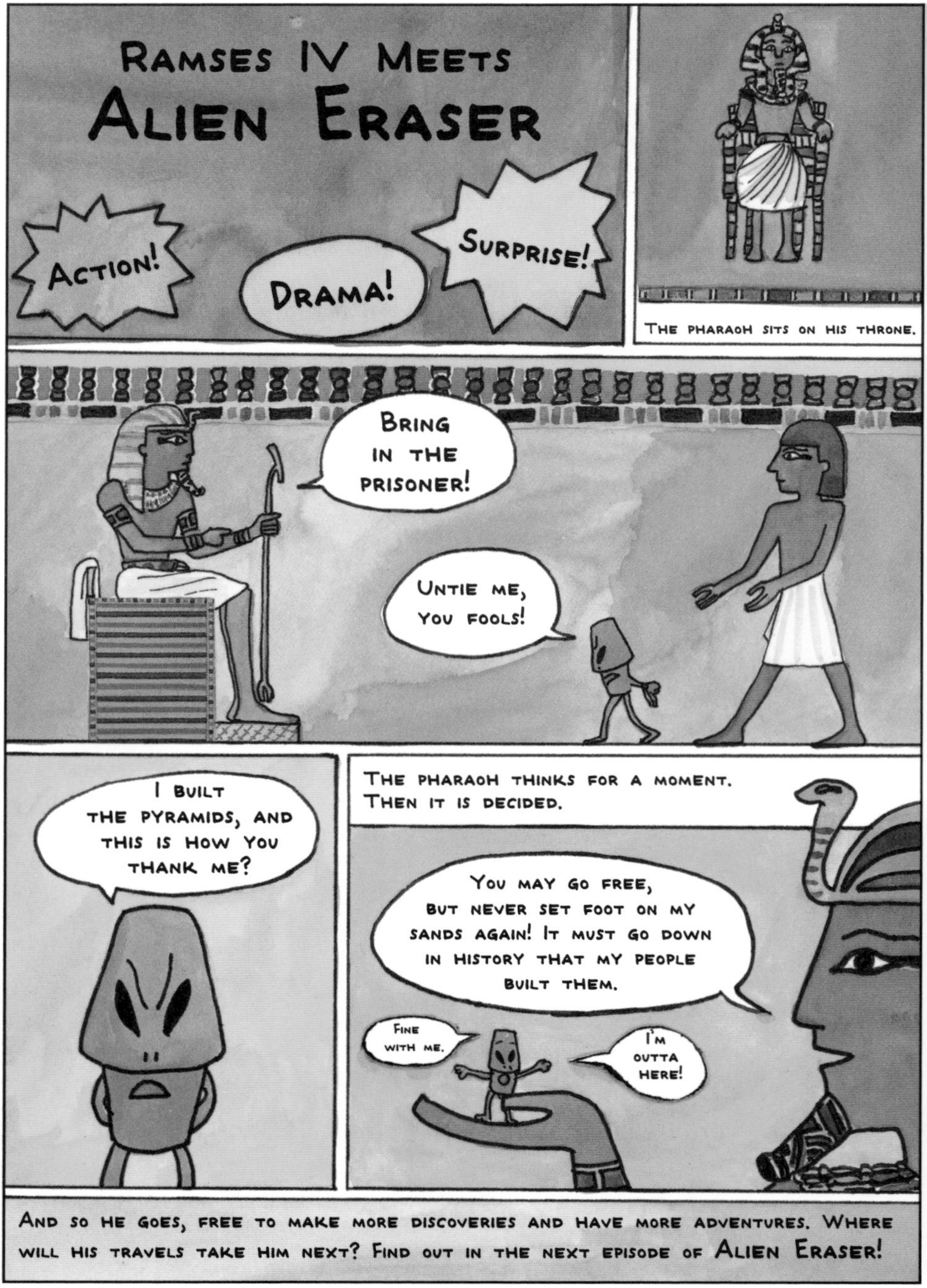
RAMSES IV MEETS
ALIEN ERASER
ACTION!
DRAMA!
SURPRISE!
THE PHARAOH SITS ON HIS THRONE.
BRING IN THE PRISONER!
UNTIE ME, YOU FOOLS!
I BUILT THE PYRAMIDS, AND THIS IS HOW YOU THANK ME?
THE PHARAOH THINKS FOR A MOMENT. THEN IT IS DECIDED.
YOU MAY GO FREE, BUT NEVER SET FOOT ON MY SANDS AGAIN! IT MUST GO DOWN IN HISTORY THAT MY PEOPLE BUILT THEM.
FINE WITH ME.
I'M OUTTA HERE!
AND SO HE GOES, FREE TO MAKE MORE DISCOVERIES AND HAVE MORE ADVENTURES. WHERE WILL HIS TRAVELS TAKE HIM NEXT? FIND OUT IN THE NEXT EPISODE OF ALIEN ERASER!

So Omar and I made a copy of the tomb painting, made a list of hieroglyphs and what they meant, and wrote a report. Then to make sure we'd get an A, we included an ancient Egyptian amulet that we made. Couldn't hurt, right?

And we didn't end up using our comics. Omar was worried about Ms. Blodge's attitude toward cartoons.

WINGED SCARAB

SCARAB CHARM—GOOD FOR POWERFUL CREATION OR CREATIVE POWER

PROTECTION AGAINST EVIL EYE AMULET

GOOD WORK, BOYS! AMAZING RESEARCH!

Ms. Blodge was impressed. The magic worked!

At back-to-school night this week, parents got to see the projects. Mom came.

Dad did, too. He loved my and Omar's project.

WELL DONE, MAX. I THOUGHT YOU WERE GOING TO DO SOMETHING ABOUT THE PYRAMID'S SUPPOSED MYSTICAL PRESERVATION PROPERTIES. THIS IS MUCH MORE INTERESTING.

WELL, YOU KNOW ME AND ALIENS.

Egypt projects by other kids:

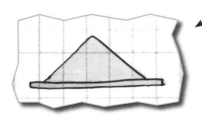

MODEL PYRAMID WITH APPLE CORE INSIDE—IT SMELLED ROTTEN! I'M GLAD WE DIDN'T DO THIS ONE.

MODEL OF SPHINX COMPLETE WITH RIDDLES—THE RIDDLES WERE THE BEST PART.

SCROLL OF RIDDLES

MODEL MUMMY MADE OF PAPIER-MÂCHÉ AND MARKERS

What? Nothing about the mummy's curse?

Egyptian snacks

PITA BREAD

HUMMUS

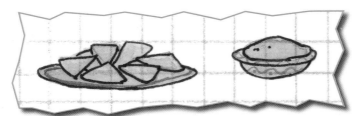

Dad took me out for ice cream afterward. It was OK, except Dad wanted to talk.

Dad had Rum Ripple. I used to wonder why they bothered making gross flavors like that, then I realized they're for grown-ups.

I had mint chocolate chip.

RUM RIPPLE

MINT CHOCOLATE CHIP

SO, ARE YOU GETTING USED TO THIS, ME NOT LIVING WITH YOU GUYS ANYMORE?

I GUESS SO.

YOU KNOW, IT'S HARD FOR ME, TOO.

I didn't say anything, but I was thinking, If it's so hard, why are you doing it?

Then a thought came to me—the reason why inventions and potions probably don't work on parents is because they are BEYOND science and magic. Sort of like aliens. They're a power unto themselves, and no matter how hard I try, I can't change them.

That wiped away all the good feelings from the ice cream and the Egypt project.

I was feeling pretty grouchy by the time Dad brought me home. I wanted him to just drop me off, but he insisted on coming in and saying hi to Kevin.

Dad really wanted Kevin's attention. Kevin just tuned him out.

Suddenly, I went from grouchy to insanely cheerful. I'd made ANOTHER discovery. I'd stumbled upon a power greater than any parents or aliens!

Who needs magic? Soon, soon, I too will have in my grasp the amazing power of . . .

THE TEENAGER!

A SUPERNATURAL FORCE TO BE RECKONED WITH

I HAVE GLIMPSED THE FUTURE, AND IT IS MINE!

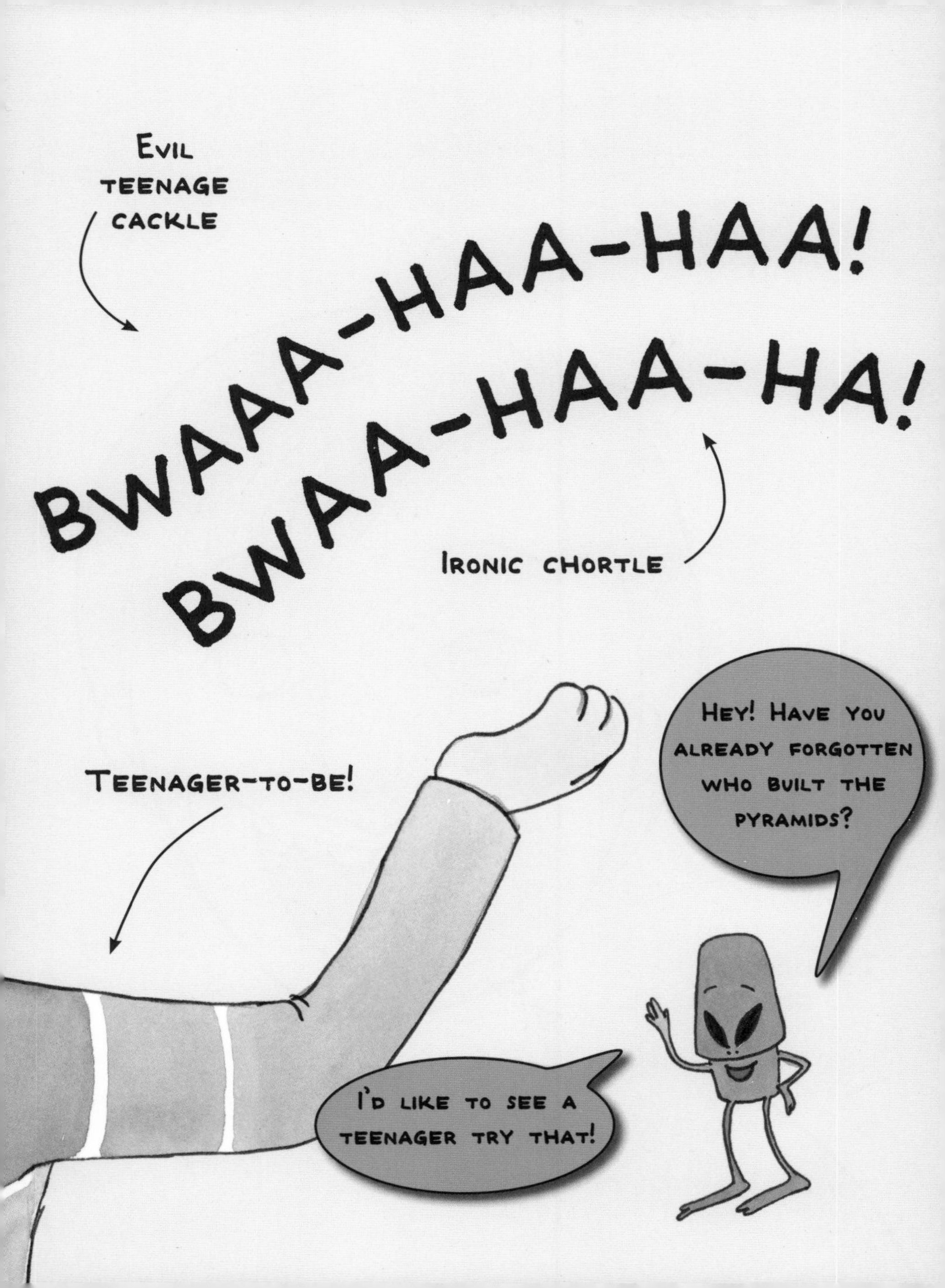
EVIL TEENAGE CACKLE
BWAAA-HAA-HAA!
BWAA-HAA-HA!
IRONIC CHORTLE
TEENAGER-TO-BE!
HEY! HAVE YOU ALREADY FORGOTTEN WHO BUILT THE PYRAMIDS?
I'D LIKE TO SEE A TEENAGER TRY THAT!

That kind of power is worth a few pimples!

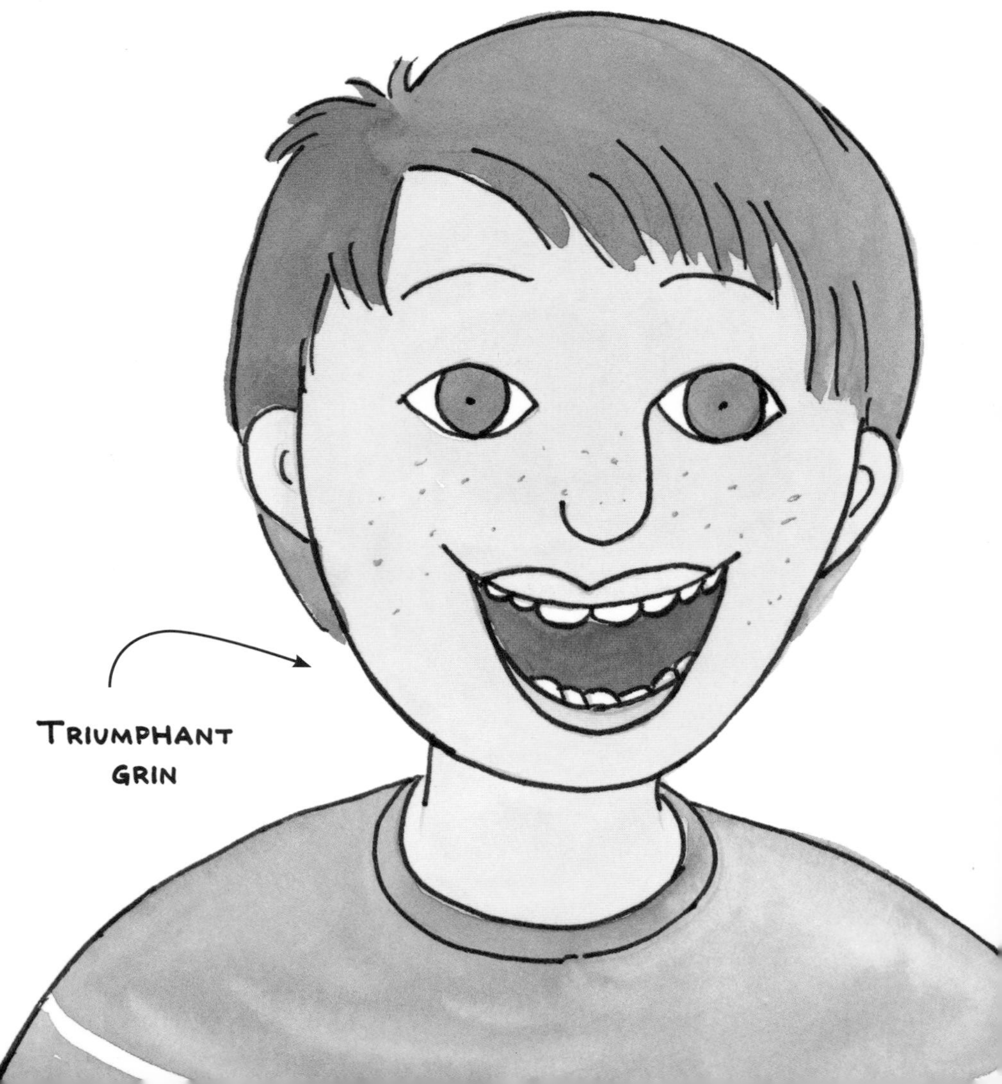
TRIUMPHANT GRIN

To Asa,

WHO STILL BELIEVES IN MAGIC

Copyright © 2009 by Marissa Moss

First Candlewick Press edition 2009

Library of Congress Cataloging-in-Publication Data is available.

Library of Congress Catalog Card Number pending

ISBN 978-0-7636-3585-5

2 4 6 8 10 9 7 5 3 1

Printed in China

This book was typeset in Kosmic Plain One, with hand-lettered type by the author-illustrator.
The illustrations were done in colored pencil, gouache, watercolor, ink, and collage.

Candlewick Press
99 Dover Street
Somerville, Massachusetts 02144

visit us at www.candlewick.com

Alien Eraser
in
The Wonders
of the
World

So far, so good. The boy has written about one of my feats.

The Great Pyramids of Egypt! A Pyramid is the perfect shape, especially once erosion wears away the pointed tip. . . .

But what about my other great achievements? I've inspired so many famous monuments.

What would Paris be without my striking profile?

Or the Golden Gate Bridge?